Danger Kid

FACING UP To Dangers
in the Home

Gianni Padoan   Illustrated by Emanuela Collini

FACING UP SERIES

Other titles

Break-up

Remembering Grandad

Follow my Leader

© 1987 Happy Books Milan Italy
English language Edition © Child's Play (International) Ltd

ISBN 0-85953-312-3
Printed in Italy

Joe and I were sitting at the edge
of the pool in the park. I yawned
and looked up at him.
"I'm bored," I said. "Why is there
nothing to do around here?"
"We could go for a ride on our bikes,"
suggested Joe.
"Not again! Let's do something
different."

"Like what?"
"I don't know. Let's go to Gwen's."
"But she'll be looking after Nicholas,"
protested Joe. "You can't do anything
with him around!"
"Why not?" I replied. "Anyway, I like
her little brother. He's fun!"
"Just remember, this was your idea,"
sighed Joe, as we jumped on our bikes.

Our mouths dropped open when Gwen opened the door.

"Wow!" Joe said. "What happened? Did Dracula get you?"
"Danger Kid, you mean!" said Gwen. "That child is a menace!"

"Don't worry," I replied. "The Seventh Cavalry is here to help!"
"Don't be too sure," said Gwen. "He's a real handful. I don't know how my parents cope!"
"It will be a piece of cake," I said. "Come on. Let's get organised!"

"Whew!" I whistled, as we went into
the sitting room. "Do your parents
allow you to be this messy?"
Gwen shook her head sadly. "No,"
she replied. "I can't stop him,
that's all."
Joe and I looked at each other.
"Just remember that this was your idea,"
he murmured. Then he shouted to Nick,
"What's all this mess? I could have
broken my leg!"

Nicholas didn't look up. "Vroom,
Vroom!" he said. "Screech! Crash!"
"I'm fed up with baby-sitting,"
moaned Gwen, collapsing into a chair.
"Come on," I said. "He's only three!"

"You just don't understand," replied Gwen. "He needs a lion-tamer, not me! I can't turn my back for a minute! And he's getting worse all the time!"
"Well, he doesn't look dangerous to me," I said.

But Gwen wasn't listening any more. "What have you got in your hands?" she screamed. "Where did you get those matches? Give them to me at once!"

"I only wanted a little fire,"
said Nick, when we had taken
the matches from him.
"But little fires become big fires,
Nick. You could burn yourself – and
the whole house too!" explained Joe
gently. "That's why you must never
play with matches."

"I'm hungry," sighed Gwen. "Who's for
lunch?"
"Me!" said Joe. "But first, let's move
things out of the way. It's dangerous
to leave them on the edge
of the worktop."

While we were getting the meal ready,
we suddenly smelled gas.
"Look what he's up to now!" I yelled.
Nick had somehow pulled open the oven
door, climbed onto it, and fiddled
with the gas taps. Now he was pushing
up the cover.
"Get off there at once!" we yelled.
"You must never climb on the oven,
and you must never touch those knobs,"
I said. "You could be badly burnt,
or scalded!"
"You know what Mum says," Gwen
joined in. "The worst accidents
in the home are when children
like you pull pans off the stove."
"Sorry," said Nick.

But a moment later, he began
to explore the cutlery drawer.

"That's enough!" said Gwen.
"Get out of the kitchen altogether!
It's not the place for you!"

Nick went off happily enough,
clutching a saucepan lid. We should
have known better.

"Mmm, this is great toast," I said.
"At last I can relax," sighed Gwen.
"Can you hear water running?"
asked Joe.

We found Nick in the bathroom.
He was leaning right over the bath,
and the tap was turned up high.

"I'm sailing my boat," said Nick,
pointing to the saucepan lid. "Look,
it's floating!"
"But you won't, if you fall in!"
yelled Gwen, as she dragged him out.
"You could bang your head and drown!"
"And suppose it had been the hot tap?"
asked Joe. "You would have scalded
yourself!"
"Sorry," said Nick. "I won't do it
again."

"Let's get you dried," said Gwen,
rubbing Nick vigorously with the
towel. Joe reached for the hairdryer.
"Joe!" said Gwen. "What an example!
You know he'll try to copy you! The
bathroom's the worst place to use
electrical things. The smallest drop
of water could electrocute you."

When Gwen had finished drying Nick with the towel, she helped Joe mop up the floor. Nick tried to open the medicine cabinet, but I stopped him. "Thanks, James," said Gwen. "But it's all right. Mum and Dad keep it locked all the time. Only they can open it."

"Let's go somewhere safe," I suggested. "I'm really tired of keeping Nick out of trouble." "It was your idea," Joe reminded me. "O.K.," agreed Gwen. "Let's go to my room and listen to records. I've just bought some new ones. Nick can't get into much trouble there." "Want to bet?" I said.

"I want this one," said Nick.
"Suppose I want this one?" answered Gwen.
"This one," repeated Nick, putting the carrier bag on his head.
"What did I tell you?" I said. "He's trying to suffocate himself now."
"Nick," said Gwen. "Please take that plastic bag off your head and give it to me."

"It's my hat!" said Nick.
"No, it's not," said Gwen. "It would stop you breathing if it went on your head any more. Never play with plastic bags."
Suddenly, a squeaky voice came from behind us. It was Joe. He had found some glove puppets.

"I am Danger Kid," squeaked a scruffy ginger-haired puppet. "See how ugly I am. I did things I was told not to do. I burnt myself on the stove. I cut myself with a knife. I fell in the bath. I put my head in a plastic bag."

Another puppet appeared, with a long white beard. "And I am Professor Safe," it said. "You musn't touch electrical sockets. Don't climb on the furniture. Don't hide in drawers and cupboards.
Don't go near the stove . . ."

But Nick was already losing interest. He wandered off. Joe put the puppets back in the box. "What do you expect?" asked Gwen. "He never sits still for more than two minutes at a time."

I watched Nick walk onto the balcony. I had a feeling that he hadn't finished with us yet.

I was right. "Help!" I yelled.
"He's climbing the railings!"
We rushed over and grabbed him.
"But I can see Annie!" he complained.
"Never mind Annie!" said Gwen.
"How many times has Dad told you
not to climb those railings?
You could easily fall and hurt yourself.
That's why Dad's putting up a net."
"Let's hope he gets it finished soon,"
said Joe.

"What shall we do next?" asked Joe.
"Let's go out," Gwen suggested.
"But what about Nick?"
"We'll take him with us," said Gwen.
"Will it be safe?" I asked.
"Of course," said Joe. "I'll keep
tight hold of him."

We hoped that the fresh air might tire Nick out. On the way, Gwen took us into the garage, to show us her new bike.

"What a super place," said Joe. "Look at all those tools!"
"I want to stay here and play!" said Nick.
"I bet you do," said Joe. "I can just imagine what you would get up to."
"He's not allowed in here," said Gwen. "He wouldn't last ten minutes."

"Come on, then," agreed Joe. "Let's go."
Before Nick could protest, Gwen swept
him up in her arms, and we set off.

Out of doors, there were lots of things
to interest Nick, so he didn't get into
mischief. All the same,
there were still things to remind him abou
"Mind the traffic, Nick!"
"Wait for the green light!"
"Look both ways!"
"Hold my hand!"

On the way home, Nick was as good
as gold. He held his new ball tightly
under one arm, and stayed close to us
all the time.
"Well done, Nick," said Joe.
"Good dog," said Nick, stretching out
a hand.
"It's dangerous to touch strange
dogs," said Gwen. "They might bite
you."

When we finally got home,
Nick was as fresh as ever,
but we were all exhausted.
"I'm shattered!" I said. "One day
with Nick is enough for me!"
"Just remember," Joe smiled. "It was
your idea . . ."